BACKHOE BANDITS

POISON

authorHOUSE®

AuthorHouse™
1663 Liberty Drive
Bloomington, IN 47403
www.authorhouse.com
Phone: 1 (800) 839-8640

Published by AuthorHouse   07/18/2016

ISBN: 978-1-5246-1900-8 (sc)
ISBN: 978-1-5246-1899-5 (e)

Library of Congress Control Number: 2016911620

Print information available on the last page.

Any people depicted in stock imagery provided by Thinkstock are models, and such images are being used for illustrative purposes only. Certain stock imagery © Thinkstock.

This book is printed on acid-free paper.

THE STORIES YOU'RE ABOUT TO READ ARE TRUE, THE FACTS ARE WRITTEN TO THE BEST OF MY KNOWLEDGE... AFTER 40 or 45 YEARS, AND SEVERAL HEAD INJURIES, SOME DETAILS MAY BE FORGOTTEN, THAT'S PROBABLY WHY THE COURTS ALLOW A STATUTE OF LIMITATIONS TO PROTECT ITS CITIZENS.

AMERICA WAS DIFFERENT SOME YEARS AGO. WE DIDN'T PAY ATTENTION TO

POLITICAL CORRECTNESS. IN FACT, THE WORD WASN'T EVEN IN OUR VOCABULARY. WE WEREN'T IGNORANT OF THE WORLD, THOUGH, SOME OF US COULDN'T EVEN READ AT A "LOWER" GRADESCHOOL LEVEL. BUT WITH GOOD WORK ETHICS, SOME OF US BECAME SUCCESSFUL IN THE TRADES WE LEARNED. AFTER ALL, IN BUSINESS, THE LAWYERS SORT EVERY LITTLE DETAIL OUT, ANYWAYS! WE PLAYED ROUGH AS KIDS, FIGHTING WAS A HIGHLIGHT OF OUR YOUTH! THERE WASN'T ANY HAZING OR INITIATION RIGHTS TO JOIN OUR "GANG"... IF YOU LIVED IN THE NEIGHBORHOOD, YOU WERE IN.

"CHUBS" THOUGHT HE WAS MORE OF A LADIES MAN, AFTER LOOSING ALOT OF WEIHT. HE BAILED ON A FEW FIGHTS THAT WE WERE IN. ONCE, EVEN HIDING UNDER A POOL TABLE WHEN GUNS WERE

DRAWN AND FIRED. DID IT MAKE ANY LESS OF A MAN OF HIM TO US? NO. WE JUST LAUGHED IT OFF! THAT WAS JUST CHUBS.

YOU WILL READ THAT STORY, TOO. SOME OF OUR "SHENANIGANS" WERE ILLEGAL, LEADING US INTO A LIFE OF CRIME. THOSE THINGS ARE RECOLLECTED IN FUZZY DETAIL, AFTER ALL, SOME OF US HAVE WORKED HARD TO BE LEGITIMATE BUSINESSMEN IN OUR COMMUNITIES. BECAUSE OF OUR FIGHT TO GO STRAIGHT, NAMES HAVE BEEN CHANGED. THIS WAS OUR PAST.

IN THE BEGINNING...

LEGITIMATE BUSINESSMEN IN OUR COMMUNITIES... That really wasn't no stretch of the imagination.

Construction has many accessible trades open to anyone with good work ethics who wants to succeed! From painters, to cement masons, and block layers, carpenters, laying tile, electricians, air conditioning, and the list even includes landscapers, pool cleaners, dry wall, stucco, "Etc., etc., etc." (as Yul Brenner said in the movie, "The King and I").

1

Sometimes, even the best of us will sin. Being there's a lot of money in the field of construction, there's also a lot of money in the black market of supplying materials for the trades. The lazy people call it "easy money", but it's not. Jail time can be a lifetime in prison. This is about a friend of mine who was addicted to the adrenaline rush of being a thief. It could have happened to any one of us, but getting married, the responsibility of a family, it was time for us to grow up, to settle down. To be men!

Even Huckleberry Finn settled down after "The Further Adventures of Huckleberry Finn", a book about his escapades during the California Gold Rush written in 1975. Read "Huckleberry Finn: Attorney-at-Law" (2015) Both are good reads!

I'm not proud of it, but I started my short life of crime by shoplifting, like most criminals. Yeah, we were criminals. The stuff didn't belong to us, we didn't pay for it, THAT makes us criminals! In some countries, our hand would be cut off!!!

Why did I shoplift? At 11 and 12 years of age, I already had a gambling addiction, playing Black Jack for toys and comic books! This way, when our parents asked where or how we got "something", truthfully, we could say we won it by playing cards; it may have been our ante, but "technically", we won it playing cards!

When I was in fifth grade, Muhammad Ali was big, "Float like a butterfly, sting like a bee." I had a reputation, for as young as I was, but it was only in my neighborhood. Kenny wanted to box with me. "No, I'm not a boxer, Ken. I'm a street fighter." He kept begging me to box with him. I said, "No."

"What's the matter? Are you chicken?"

"Okay, put on the gloves."

Kenny peppered me with punches to my face, I covered up. Four times he peppered me with 15 or 16 punches to my face. I kept covering up with my gloves. I only threw one punch. I hit him so hard, it knocked him down, and Kenny had a headache for three days!

We grew bolder with our crimes as we grew older. To me, Simon was an all together special friend; I owed him my life. THAT story's later.

Simon was arrested for burglary. He was convicted because of HALF a thumbprint! While serving time, every day he was released in the yard to "exercise", all he did was run in the yard. Finally, one night, he escaped! He ran more than 30 miles to get home! The police were waiting in the living room when he opened the door at home.

As a result, Simon had to serve MORE TIME FOR ESCAPE! At 5;10", 240 pounds, Simon was a beefy, muscular young man. Once in a fight, he body slammed the guy onto the hard sidewalk! We didn't mess around when we got into fights! Rarely we needed weapons.

I said "rarely", because, one time, I remember us going to a go-cart ring. And we were driving go-carts, racing, innocent fun. The lot attendant signaled to us our rides were over. A couple of us pulled out, but Ted kept racing. The kid told him a second time, a third time, then he told his boss. The manger told him a second, and third time to pull out. Finally, after his fourth or fifth trip around the race track, the manager stood in front, ON THE RACETRACK, to stop him! Ted stopped. That was when the manager hit Ted over the head with his clipboard! Bad mistake. They both stood up and started fighting. The manager had his back to me, and I gunned my engine to run him over. After all, it was just a go-cart!

Ted threw a punch and they changed places. I ended up running over Ted instead.

While my go-cart was on top of Ted, he was on the ground, the manager kicked Ted in the ribs. Somehow, Alvin produced a hickory ax handle, and tossed it to Ted. After that, I remember seeing that manager holding up his right arm, to prevent Ted from busting him over the head with that hickory ax handle. I'm sure his arm was broken.

We got in fights all the time!

Just out of sixth grade, I got into my first gang fight. It was seven kids against Rick and I. Their leader had a bike chain with a padlock on the end of it.

He swung it at me, it was so heavy, when I stepped back, I noticed he was off his balance. The second time he swung the chain at me, I stepped back, when he was off balance, I attacked him. I threw a headlock on him, and sat on the hot pavement, in the middle of the summer in Phoenix, in my bare feet and cut-offs, with his head in my lap, hitting him.

My dad jumped out of the car and tried to help me! I growled at him, and said, "He's mine!" My dad stepped back, got in the car and watched.

After several hits, his amigo, with a bike kickstand in his hand, told me to let him go. I looked at him, smiled and hit his friend three more times. When I saw that kickstand coming down like a hatchet, I ducked my head. That's when Rick got in the fight. He hit somebody, by that time, my assailant got away, my feet were burning on the hot pavement. I saw somebody running up behind Rick, swinging that chain over his head for momentum, and I couldn't yell a warning. The kid wrapped that bike chain around Rick's head, and the lock hit him. Rick grabbed the chain, pulled the kid towards him and knocked him out.

And while this was going on, about eight or ten senior citizens stood and cheered us on! Was it because these kids were from the projects? I don't know. I like to think it was because it was two against seven! We weren't raised to be prejudice. After their hearing a second call from the store's loudspeakers to call the police, those kids ran off. I never did see any cops come. My dad asked if we wanted a ride home, I said, "No, we'll walk." When we got to Rick's house, we told his mom about the fight, that's when they noticed my back was bleeding. I had so much adrenalin going through my veins, I didn't notice, I didn't feel any pain!

Like I said, we weren't raised to be prejudice. Don and I were the fastest kids in the school we went to in seventh grade, even faster than all of the eighth graders! I finally beat him on Field Day in eighth grade. Once, I brought Don home to meet my family. I opened the front door and stuck my head in, my mom was sitting at the dining room table and I said, "Hey, Mom! Guess who's coming over for dinner?"

Don stuck his head in the doorway and said, "Hi, mom!" my mom burst out laughing! This was around the time the movie, GUESS WHO'S COMING TO DINNER with Sidney Poitier came out.

Once, Ted and I were driving down a two lane street, Alvin's brother, "Bingo", tried to pass us. Ted sped up. We were going 60 miles an hour, cars were pulling off the road to avoid head-on collisions. That was the one and only time I was ever scared being with Ted. Silly me, cars weren't going to get in OUR LANE to avoid a collision! That road has two lanes going in each direction, and a center lane, now.

Another time, the two of us were going down the street, a hippie crossed the street TWO BLOCKS

IN FRONT OF US! A good one hundred yards! Ted pulled up next to him in a parking lot, grabbed him by the shirt, and paint brushed him 8 or 9 times, slapping both sides of his face! Ted said, "Are you ever going to do that, again?" The guy was slapped silly!

In a groggy state, he said, "Yeah, yeah... I mean, no! No! Not if this is going to happen!" Ted slapped him a few more times and dropped him on the asphalt. Ted got back in the station wagon and we left.

We drove a couple blocks, AND I SWEAR I WAS BEING SARCASTIC, I said, "Gee, Ted! You let that guy off easy!"

Ted immediately made a U-turn, went back into that parking lot! The hippie saw him and ran into a liquor store to get away!

The liquor store owner started yelling, "Don't trash my store! Don't trash my store!" Ted dragged the hippie out by the hair and slapped him another half dozen times and drops him on the cement sidewalk. This is the same Ted that, years later, TWICE donated a 55 gallon drum of paint to paint a church. Ted was always the giver, even AFTER we reached drinking age, he always bought the beer.

The first time I went to Alvin's house, we went horseback riding. Alvin saddled his sister's horse for me and we rode through the orange orchards. Towards the end of our ride, Alvin was about thirty yards ahead, talking to his mom in her car, and I kicked THE SIDES of my horse to catch up. The saddle slid to the side of the horse. Spooked, the horse started to bolt towards a busy street a hundred yards away. Alvin's mom yelled, "Saddle burn!" I really didn't want to be in that situation, so I let go of the reins, and dropped onto a somewhat paved, potholed street. While Alvin raced after us, he caught up and calmed the horse.

What made these guys accept me, immediately, I got back on the horse after Alvin double-checked the saddle. The problem was, the horse didn't like Alvin. Probably because it was his sister's horse, he looked at her funny, he yelled at her, who knows what goes in a horses head. I'm not a "horse whisperer". When she was being saddled, the horse took a deep breath in protest. This made the saddle loose. The next day, we rode the same horses, again. As we rode through the grapefruit orchards, again, that was next to the Chinese flower farm where I later proposed to my wife on the canal bank, I kicked her to catch up, another saddle burn! The horse tried scraping me off her back by brushing against the tree branches. At a twenty foot square space where a tree was dug out, I let go and ate the dirt! But, I got right back on her after Alvin caught her. They saw I knew no fear. I knew fear, it's just I wasn't very acquainted with it.

Alvin and Mario were both chasing after the same girl. Alvin took it personally. They got in a fight, Mario drew first blood from Alvin. Alvin went insane! He almost drowned Mario in the irrigated lawn in the girls front yard. Mario was yelling, "HELP! Blub, blub, blub... HELP! Blub, blub, blub.... HELP!blub, blub,

blub." We had to pull Alvin off of him to keep him from drowning Mario.

One night after Mario's near drowning, Alvin, his future wife, and I went to a seedy part of town known as "Dog town". I don't know what the reason was, maybe Alvin wanted to show her off or something. We were talking to three guys, and five more showed up. Then, two more. Then some big dude named Hershel came out and started to challenge Alvin to a fight. We both had our hands on the door handles, Rene was begging Alvin not to fight. Then somebody reached in the car window and punched Alvin in the mouth. We both jumped out of the car. Two guys fought Alvin, because he already had a reputation. The rest of them jumped on me!

Hershel grabbed me in a bear hug, pinning my arms to my side. I punched him, but I couldn't get any power in my punches because I couldn't swing! This was the first time I was ever being whooped in a fight! So, I bit him on the chest! He let go, I ran about ten yard to, put my hands on my knees to shake the cobwebs out of my head and started to run back in the fight... and everybody disappeared!

Alvin pulled out a gun! People were hiding behind trees, bushes, garbage cans, Alvin aimed that .45, "Alvin! It ain't worth it!" I yelled. "We'll get them back some other time!" Alvin kept that pistol on his target... "Alvin, don't. They ain't worth going to jail for. We'll get 'em back some other day. Come on. Let's go." He finally lowered the gun and got back in the car. We drove about 30 yards and they reappeared, being illuminated under a street light, like the cockroaches they were.

Alvin stopped the car and got out, aiming, again. Again, they disappeared.

I said, "Alvin! They ain't worth going to jail over. We'll get 'em back some other day!" Alvin held that gun on them for about thirty more seconds before he put it down this time. Alvin took me home and I turned the yard hose on and washed off. My mom came outside and asked, "What happened to you?"

I said, "Oh, the car was still moving when I got out and I bit the dust." Assessing my injuries, I had two black eyes a fat lip and four bumps on my back the size of an open palm of the back of my hand. That ain't so bad, knowing it took nine of them, and that was all the damage they did.

The fun I had growing up with the old neighborhood kids and the fun I had with my high school friends were like two different worlds. A couple times, I heard Ted, Simon, and Alvin talk about playing "*Broom*". This "game", the idea was to drive down the main street, if somebody was walking down the street, you'd drive by and hit them in the back of the head with a broom. The point of the game was, if you dropped the broom, you had to go back BY YOURSELF to get it!

My high school friends decided to "play". We went up and down Central, the guys in the back of the truck swung at a couple dozen people, AND THEY

ALWAYS MISSED! This got boring, so we decided to go home. While driving home, we saw three big hippies hitch-hiking the other direction. I was sitting shotgun and, excited, I yelled, "Go back, go back!" We turned around in a church parking lot, and drove back to them.

As we slowed down, the hippies started cheering, they thought they finally got a ride. With one swing, I hit the first one in the stomach, the second one in the chest and the third one in the face, knocking all three of them down. These guys were big, biker type men. Mike, Jim and somebody else were leaning out of the back of the truck READY TO CATCH THAT BROOM IN CASE I DROPPED IT. We laughed all the way home.

Once, we were driving down the road, some 19 or 20 year old man was walking, going in the same direction. Ted pulled over, slammed his brakes on in the dirt, reached in the back of the truck, grabbed an ax, and ran at this kid! This guy must have thought he knew kung fu. He got into his self defense stance, waving his arms like he knew what he was doing, Ted was getting closer with that ax over his head, ready to swing it, I'm in the back of the truck, yelling, "Kill him, Ted! Kill him!" The kid had second thoughts about it, he turned around and ran. Ted wouldn't have killed him, it was for laughs! Even if he would have stood his ground, Ted, probably would have just slapped him "paintbrush" style, like that hippie in the parking lot.

Of all the years I've known Ted, he's only been whooped once. He was drinking in a biker bar. They beat him into a conscienceless concussion. To this day, he'll drink, then pretend he's passed out, asleep, listening to the conversation. He knows who his friends are this way. He's been in **hundreds** of fights. On a good day, maybe two or three! This Ultimate Fighting Championship stuff is about 40 years too late for him. Ted was the best I've ever seen. Twice he's had gangrene in his fists from fights. Now, after he knocks you down, he'd put the boot to you! Kenny took me to a couple

Ultimate Fighting fights. I fell asleep at both of them. I was so bored by the "entertainment". BOREING!

I would never challenge Ted in a fight. It's not fear, I had THAT MUCH respect for him. I was a powerhouse myself when I was younger. (At the age of 17, I did a repetition of ten full squats with **640 pounds** of loose weight, NOT on a machine.

On the *Universal Weight Machine* six weeks before, I did the 750 pound maximum on the leg press a repetition of 75 times! I stopped because I was laughing too hard at a bigger man, David "Killa McCalla" McCalla, who challenged me after my snickering at his feeble attempt, who couldn't do it once. At 5'6", 145 pounds, I was doing several reps with that kind of weight since I was **13 years old**!) We had Olympic weights, but it wasn't an Olympic weight barbell. The way I'd "pop" back up, the barbell bent! It was funny! David's counting the reps, "7, 8, 9, 10..." the machine was shaking like it was going to fall apart... "37, 38, 39, 40, All right Poison., you proved your point,... 62, 63, 64, 65..., ALL RIGHT, POISON.,... 72, 73, 74, 75."

It was the school record, the 640 pound squats, for more than a year! The AIA "(Arizona, Interscholastic Association) put a stop with that kind of extreme weight to protect the high school athlete. If the bar snapped, it would have cut me off at the knees! Now, the school records throughout the state only have a 610 pound maximum.

Alvin, on the other hand, I was laying down on the carpet in the front room, watching cartoons one Saturday morning when Alvin blew some marijuana smoke in my face. None of us guys DID drugs! I told him to knock it off. He did it a second time and I popped him in the jaw. I stood up and said, "I told you to stop!" He treated me like a boxing speed bag! He must have hit me, throwing 16 to 20 punches at me. Ted and Simon had to stop him! No, I wasn't bleeding.

While talking to his mom about our "fight", Alvin, with tears in his eyes, asked his mom, "Why do we have to grow up?"

We all went to a bar one night because they were having "Bar Room Brawling". A boxing ring was brought in and the patrons could sign up, and they'd match you with somebody of similar size and age. All of us signed up, then we found out, after the gloves were put on me, that they had no more trophies. Ted said, "Let's go home. They ran out of trophies." But, me, adrenaline was already pumping in my veins! "Not me, I'm fightin'!" I said. Ted was bummed because they ran out of trophies, it wasn't worth it. The trophies were what drew us to THAT bar in the first place! "No, lets go, there's no more trophies," Ted repeated. At least one other guy, some college kid, about 6'1", told Ted, "Let the man decide for himself." He already had the gloves on, so I guess he thought he could take me, being more half than a foot shorter. Ted didn't like his smart-alack remark, NOW, Ted wanted to fight him and tried taking my gloves off. I wrapped my arms around my body and said, "No, he's mine!"

Ted volunteered to be in my corner as my second. The bell rang for the FIRST ROUND to begin. This kid peppered me! I covered up, protecting myself. We separated, that clown had four girls in his corner as his seconds, cheering him on! A second and third time, that kid peppered me with a flurry of head shots! We kept separating, the fourth time we met in the center of the ring, I finally threw my first punch, a left round house. I hit him so hard, he was on his back! A standing ten count. He threw a couple more flurry's on me before the bell rang.

SECOND ROUND: The kid threw another flurry of punches on me, I covered up. When we met, again, I threw another left round house, he went down, AGAIN! Standing ten count, he threw another flurry on me, THEN HE KICKED ME! He got his FIRST warning. He threw two more flurry's on me. Finally, I threw my third round house, and I knocked him down,

AGAIN! I only threw three punches by this time. Technically, he lost after the third knock down, but everybody wanted to see this little guy knocking down this big guy! We met again, and HE KICKED ME A SECOND TIME! He got a SECOND warning just before the bell rang ending the SECOND round.

Ted, in my corner, told me, "As soon as the bell rings, run over there and knock that idiot out while he's still in his corner! You can end this fight THAT quick!" The bell rang to start the third round, and I sprinted across the ring! He was still sitting on his chair as I stood over him with my fist raised, ready to knock him out. HE KICKED ME A THIRD TIME! I was so focused, I didn't see the flag they threw in as I ran across the ring. He gave up. I won! Kicking me a third time, technically, he lost, again! Ted was STILL mad at him! Ted ran around the ring into his corner, and with one punch, knocked him out! Because my second hit the other fighter, I was disqualified.

But, that's all right, they didn't have any more trophies, anyway. But, we had fun!

Simon would "repo" a three or four ton truck and we'd load it with a hundred or two sheets of plywood, or refrigerators, or air conditioners. Once, I was on lookout. They said I fell asleep! I don't remember. It was STILL a successfully profitable night, I don't even remember if I got my cut, it didn't matter. There was always money ANOTHER night.

Then there was the *Scorpion Gulch* fight. It always brought fond memories if it was mentioned when we were all together.

Ted and I were home with no plans for that evening. Alvin called. "You better get down here, and hurry. It looks like there's going to be trouble." We rushed down there. As we walked in, somebody said, "Oh, look! Here comes the cavalry!"

There was Ted, Alvin, Chubs, Simon and I against seven guys. Blows were thrown, and two of our rivals pulled out their guns! Chubs immediately hid under a pool table! Just as quick, Alvin reached for one of the guns and locked his finger in the hammer to prevent it from firing. He hit the guy a couple of times, he wouldn't let go of the gun.

So I applied, or tried to apply, a police disarmament move, called "a fish hook". The idea was to put your finger in the assailant's mouth and pull their cheek out, avoiding their teeth and being bitten! The pain is mindbogglingly severe! The assailant will comply with ANYTHING the officer says.

The problem was, my finger didn't go in his mouth. I couldn't see what I was doing. Alvin was in my way. My finger went in this guy's eye! I said, "Let go of the gun!"

He said, "No!"

I dug my finger in his eye, popping it out! I said, "LET GO OF THE GUN!"

"Okay, okay!"

The other gun was pointed at Ted, and he ran along the bar behind the counter. Five or six shots were fired. The lava rock wall behind the counter splattered shrapnel in Ted's back. Ted ducked into the office and searched the desk hoping to find a gun. He couldn't even find a letter opener, so he improvised; he grabbed the only weapon in there... a couple of 2 liter bottles of Coca- Cola! 2 liter bottles were made out of thick glass bottles back then!

Tom stuck his head out the door, saw somebody with their back to him, so Ted smacked him in the back of the head with a full 2 liter bottle, knocking him out. He hurried onto the dance floor, and slipped in the blood from the guy who's eye I just took out. As he was falling, he crashed that other bottle on the head of somebody else. I think this is where Simon body slammed two guys on the dance floor.

Somebody tried running out the door, Ted followed them and threw a beer bottle through the back window of their truck as they pulled out on the street. When he got back in the bar, Alvin had four guys lined up against the bar. Each one, with the pistol in his hand, he said,

"Admit it, you bit off more than you guys could chew today, didn't you?"

"Yeah", said the first guy.

"Admit it, you bit off more than you guys could chew, today, didn't you?"

"Yeah", said the second guy.

"Admit it, you guys bit off more than you could chew, today, didn't you?"

"Yeah", said the third guy.

"Admit it, you guys bit off more than you could chew, today, didn't you?"

"F@#% you!" said the fourth guy.

Alvin pistol whipped him as he slammed the handle of that pistol into his jaw, knocking out several teeth as they rolled onto the bar floor.

After the police arrived, Ted helped a cop pull Chubs out from under the pool table! He was still stuck under there. We left him there because it was something to laugh about to relieve the tension.

We had to sign statements for the police when they got there. When I signed my statement, my hand was shaking so bad, I couldn't even read my own signature! We never did go to court over the incident. It was self defense.

SETTELIN' DOWN

When I met my future bride, I brought her home to introduce to Ted, my prize, whose heart I had just won. Ted introduced me to his old girlfriend, Jamie. Now it was my turn for introductions: "Hi, Jamie. Ted, this is... ahhh...um... ahhh..." There immediately was too much dead air.

"JANICE!"

"Yeah. This is Janice." (Hey, she married me, anyways.)

A week later I took her home to meet my mom and my little brother. Immediately, she and my little brother took off in my truck. I didn't know where or why. They just "hit it off" THAT quick! I wasn't worried, I trusted them both.

That night, Janice said she knew how much I loved my little brother, and that I was against drug abuse; my brother, being a block layer, asked her where he could get some speed. Man, I was mad! I didn't say anything, I stood up and walked into the room addition, enclosing Ted's garage that we were installing, and Janice said, "Don't do anything stupid." I punched the dry wall hanging on the walls, punching it about twenty times.

Four or five times I hit a stud, a 2x4 behind the sheet rock, breaking my hand. It was swollen, the optimist that I am, I thought it was just dislocated; it didn't hurt. I thought when Ted got home that night, he'd reset it, pulling it back into place. Ted thought it was broken, too. It was swollen so bad, the E.R. doctor told me I'd have to wait 3 days before they could set it. I never did take anything for pain. Three days later, as the doctor reset it, putting on the cast, he said, "You have a high tolerance for pain."

"What do you mean, doc?"

"I'm setting your hand, you didn't even blink your eyes!" My oldest daughter didn't receive a tolerance for pain from my genes.

Sandi was about 5 or 6 years old, playing on a playhouse across the street from my mom. She climbed up on top of the 8 foot roof, slipped, and rolled off and broke her arm. My mom took her to the Emergency Room, and a doctor reset it. She was screaming bloody murder, it hurt so bad.

As the doctor was putting on a cast, Sandi was sniveling, "Ow, ow, oweee... Ow, ow, oweee... Ow, ow, oweee," (to me, when my mom told me the story, I thought it was cute!)

When Janice was eight months pregnant with our first son, I didn't have the backbone to marry her. We went to *Dairy Queen*, and we both got strawberry sundaes. As we sat down, I stood up, again. "I'll be right back"

"Where are you going?" she asked.

"I'll be right back." Quickly, I went to the grocery store next door, bought a can of sardines, and opened it up and dumped the contents on my strawberry sundae. It tasted fine to me. That was the first and only time I ever ate sardines that day. (Janice always craved *Kitkat* candy bars when she was pregnant.)

Two years after our divorce, just after her birthday in January, Janice was living in Albuquerque, I was living 750 miles away; I hadn't even really seen her for well over a year, and I got another craving for sardines! I ate one can, had no desire for the second. I called her that night, and I asked her, "Are you pregnant?"

"No, I'm not pregnant! It's none of your f%@^*#> business! Get out of my life!" She was still cussing me, when I hung up the phone. In August of that same year, our kids got a new baby half-sister.

When Sandi was 21, I took a 72 ½ hour vacation to see all 4 of our kids, (swing through Wyoming and visit Salt Lake City and Las Vegas). As I got in my truck to leave her house, I asked Sandi how soon they would be having kids. "Oh, not for another 4 or 5 years," Sandi said.

When I got back home, my first day back at work, I craved sardines! For three days at work I ate sardine sandwiches at lunch! A couple months later, I found out both Spartan AND Sandi were expectant parents! (I always thought that Sandi was probably working on it as I was backing out of her driveway! But, THAT'S just the conspiracy theorist in me.)

Ted and I, our oldest sons are about a year apart. They were playing in his driveway, Spartan was 4 ½ years old, a little older than little Ted. Big Ted was watching them play on his driveway while sitting in a lawn chair, drinking a beer. I looked out front the window and saw my son on the ground and little Ted "putting the boot" to him, kicking him while he was down. Kids don't do that naturally. Ted was teaching it to his son! I was furious! I called my son to come home, "NOW"! When my son got home, I told him, "When little Ted wants to fight, tell him "No." If he tries to pick a fight a second time, tell him, "No." If he tries to pick a fight a third time, punch him in the nose, push him down on the ground, grab him by the ears and bang his head into the ground, punch him in the nose, again and tell him to go home."

A week later, little Ted tried picking a fight. My son did as he was told. The result: little Ted was so traumatized, one of Ted's workers had to carry him home from our yard across the street! Oh, boy, Ted was mad! "If you're going to teach your son to fight, I'll teach my son how to fight, too!" Ted yelled!

I yelled back, "You DID teach little Ted how to fight! A kid doesn't naturally kick another kid when he's down! He would jump on him!" THAT ended the argument, because Ted knew I knew how HE fights.

Twice Ted got gangrene in his fist from fights with people who weren't too familiar with tooth brushes and what they were suppose to be used for!

A couple weeks later, the kids were playing in our house, my wife was cleaning our son's room. She asked little Ted to do something and he turned around and cussed my wife out. Man, she was mad!

She said, "Spartan! Tare him apart!" My son beat little Ted's head in on the linoleum floor, this time! Little Ted ran home crying, saying my wife beat him up.

Ted was mad! I told him, "He's lying! He didn't want to get in trouble because Spartan beat him up for cussing out Janice!" That was the last I heard of it, little Ted must have admitted it.

I'm off subject, now, I apologize.

Being in construction, we knew what people needed who were doing side jobs. I first supplied them by "acquiring" scores of 2x4's, I was paid $100. But, there was more money in plywood.

Sometimes, I noticed a favorite song on the radio, if I heard it, I noticed we'd have a "successful" night. We started doing "repo's" on nights I heard that song, it was "like magic".

In time, we all married good women. That led us into being productive citizens. But, some people still enjoyed the adrenaline rush in thieving.

One night, our wives met to attend a Tupperware party. Innocent enough? The husbands went to a bar. After some beers, we started drinking daiquiri's. When they ran out of strawberries and orange's, we drank banana daiquiri's.

At 8:45 that night, we all headed back to the Tupperware party in two vehicle's, along with a "kid" we met, we knew his big brother. Racing to one house to drop somebody off, one of us pulled a big green garbage can in the middle of the road, in front of the "kid". He hit it, it flew, we all laughed.

A couple blocks from the party, I told the driver, "Pull over, pull over!" He pulled over and I got out and pulled another big green garbage can in the middle of the road. That's all I remember. They said I was hiding behind it when the "kid's old pickup truck hit it. I flew about fifty feet. All my friends, my "brothers", left me for dead, there, except Simon. Men I grew up with! This is the debt I owed my friend, Simon. People, hearing the brakes screech and the impact, wandered outside to see what happened. Simon yelled at them, "Get in the house! He's okay! He's okay! GET BACK IN YOUR HOUSE!"

I was "blessed" with a high tolerance for pain. When I came to a minute later, I limped up behind him and put my hand on his shoulder. He turned around with his fist balled up ready to knock me out, again. He didn't know I was still alive! I said, "Come on! Let's get out of here!" Simon helped me to the nearest alley, about fifty yards away.

After passing 3 or 4 houses, he said, "Wait here, I'll see if Chubs is home." Simon climbed a six foot cyclone fence and knocked on the back door. Chubs answered.

Meanwhile, I'm in the alley thinking, "I've gotta get out of here!" I thought we were in trouble for something. So, with a broken knee from the impact, I climbed that six foot cyclone fence to meet up with Simon and Chubs at the back door in the back yard.

"MEANWHILE, BACK AT THE RANCH..."

At the Tupperware party, Janice, my wife, overheard some of the guys say, "What do you think happened to him?"

"I don't know."

"I don't know, I think he's dead."

Instantly worried, AND nine months pregnant, Janice asked, "Where's **POISON**.?

"Hey, he's okay."

Janice yelled, "WHERE'S **POISON**.?"

So, all the husbands climbed back in the trucks to look for me. They saw an ambulance driving up and down the street real slow, they asked the driver, "Where are you taking him?"

The medic said, "I don't know! I haven't found anyone, yet!" When they returned to the Tupperware party, I was sitting down because my knee hurt. We all decided I SHOULD go to the emergency room. The nearest hospital was less than a mile away. I had my wife drive to a hospital more than twenty miles away. Not in the next town, but in the town on THE OTHER SIDE of the next town, two towns away! Like I said, I thought I was in trouble for something. Blame it on being drunk on daiquiri's and another possible head injury.

When we pulled up to the emergency room, a local police car was already there looking for me, or for a body from that incident because that medic couldn't find me.

When the cop saw me limping to the emergency room, he asked me what happened. "Oh, I was drinking and my wife was driving us home. She turned a corner and I fell out of the truck." That satisfied his curiosity. This was the first time I broke my knee.

Sometimes, we still got together, once for a softball game a couple of years later, after "my accident". The accident should have left me crippled for life, several people died, it was THAT bad. (Nobody was ticketed because the other driver, who died, had alcohol in his blood. My blood was clean. I only drank once a month or two after I married.) That's the prognosis the doctor gave me. I asked him how soon I'd be able to walk, again. He said, "You'll never be able to walk, again, unless it's with a cane."

My response to him, was, "Well, I heal real quick."

That softball game was the last time I saw a successful friend of ours who's funeral I later went to. THAT story is just ahead.

I met that "kid" again, a few years later. We were moving into that house across the street from Ted, who was helping us paint the inside before moving our furniture in. Ted said, "Yeah, you guys met before! This is the "kid" that ran you over that night!"

The "kid" started laughing, recalling that night. I got mad, I didn't want to mess up the walls we just painted, so I went outside to wash the paint from the brushes and rollers. That kid followed me, still laughing about the incident. I jumped on him!

I bent his arm so far behind his back, I dislocated his shoulder and probably his elbow, too. When I let go of him, he walked off cussing me, vowing revenge. His arm was still behind his back, he couldn't even bring it to his side.

THE BACKHOE BANDITS

Simon got in trouble, again. This is where things are sketchy. I lost touch with everybody for years after my divorce. Now, this is my own witness, word of mouth from friends, relatives, in-laws and out-laws. I could search for public records. THAT WOULD MAKE THIS INFORMATION ALL LEGAL, BUT MAYBE, this is MY adrenaline rush. Not gossip, facts gathered first hand. To me, Simon needed his case pleaded.

After several years of us not being all together, Simon and Alvin still hung out, or, rather, "worked" together. While I was "hooking' an' crookin'", selling frozen steak, chicken and seafood door- to-door, Simon ALLEGIBLY ran a car theft ring along with Alvin, PROBABLY.

At least THAT was one of the charges he was convicted of.

Allegedly, from what I heard, an accomplice thought he was being cheated, and threatened to turn Simon in. The spineless would-be-tattle-tail was run over by a truck.

Unconscious, under the truck, Simon ALLEGEDLY opened the oil pan valve and drained all the hot oil on the chest of the would-be-snitch. Because of THAT AND other charges, Simon received a 295 year prison sentence with no chance for parole.

Basically, a life sentence. Right?

Because there's a lot of idle time in prison, men talk about their successes, their past, how "bad" they were on the outside in hopes of getting respect on the inside. Even talking about what crimes they got away with to show how "good" or how "smart" they were.

Al Capone went to the grave proclaiming his innocence. He saw himself as nothing but a public benefactor. A man who only gave the public what they wanted. Even his business card said he was a used furniture dealer! In his legacy, he started the **B.B.B.** The **Better Business Bureau**. I'm sure, somewhere in a basement or the archives of the **B.B.B.** in Chicago, there's a picture of Al Capone, smiling, wearing a white fedora hat with the caption under his picture, saying, "OUR FOUNDER".

Because Simon's sentence was so steep, EVERYBODY KNEW HE'D NEVER SEE FREEDOM, AGAIN. One man, bragging about the crimes he got away with, told Simon how he did it!

Simon went to the warden to make a deal. He'd get the taped confession in exchange for his freedom. The deal was made. Simon got the confessions. Simon got his freedom.

Simon was only out for a month, and at a bar-b-q, ol' Lester, one of our dear brothers, mentioned how he'd like to mess with Simon's sister in a physical way. Apparently, she was one of the few people who would visit him in prison. I at least wrote him a few times, he kept asking for money, They give you everything you physically need in jail. I knew he wasn't one to be pushed around in there. He didn't need my money THAT bad!

Enraged, Simon beat Lester almost to death. Simon beat him up so severely, the judge sentenced him to another ten years in prison, saying he was a habitual criminal. Simon did his time, this time. In all, by the time he was forty five, he spent more than half his life incarcerated.

As a dog returneth to his vomit, *so* a fool returneth to his folly. Proverbs 26:11

Simon and Alvin started a new enterprise: stealing backhoe's to steal ATM machines. I remember reading in the local newspaper two incidents, NOT KNOWING IT WAS THEM, my friends.

Why steal ATM machines? Clyde Barrow of the Bonnie and Clyde fame was asked the same question, "Why do you rob banks?"

He replied, "Because that's where the money is!"

One cold, moonless night, they stole another backhoe. While speeding across the desert on that moonless night, in the dark, probably at 20 to 25 miles per hour, Simon, while not wearing the seat belt, crashed into a gully, a desert dry wash. Obviously, Simon was severely injured.

Alvin, probably following him in a pickup truck as a getaway vehicle (to load the ATM machine in), probably, with tears in his eyes, loaded Simon in the truck and drove down a canal to assess his injuries. Alvin always said that he would NEVER go to jail. I believe, Alvin probably knocked Simon out (maybe with an uppercut, or kicking him in the chin), and, with tears in his eyes, rolled him into the canal, putting him out of his misery. He was afraid Simon might talk. Why tears? They played and rode horses together before they were in GRADE SCOOL! Over 45 years ago.

Because some of their exploits with ATM's sounds so incredible, Just now, I retrieved some of the news paper articles, (INFORMATION THAT WAS EVEN NEW TO ME!) to verify my story:

XXXXXXXXXXXXXXXXXXXXXXX

XXXXXXXXXXXXXXXXXXXXXx

They found Simon a month later, after his being reported missing, dead, tangled in the irrigation gates with the debris, tires, bottles and who knows what else people throw in the canal when it was drained. When I was told of Simon's death about a year later, Ted and I both said at the same time, "Alvin did it."

Ted must have told his wife of the coincidence of our suspicions in front of his kids.

Alvin covered his tracks well, even leaving an alibi with the ATV in the area where the body was found MORE THAN 25 MILES AWAY from his home. That is, **IF ALVIN DID WHAT WE SUSPECTED!** DNA at the accident scene must have surely been taken from the blood loss Simon suffered, thus identifying his involvement with the stolen backhoe, creating suspicions and possibly re-opening the possibility of Simon's drowning in the canal, pointing to an accomplice. The trouble is, law agencies don't share their information easily, even after their failures in 9/11.

The ATM targeted may have PROBABLY been in Scottsdale or Cave Creek, Arizona. Hitting Mesa, AGAIN, would have been too risky, especially if they heard of the failed attempt of the two men that did the ATM job a mile away from their first job, on the news. I'm sure the ATV, with no fresh fingerprints, was planted several miles, maybe even a couple towns away from where the backhoe was found. I use to have a thieving mindset, but I left that life years ago. That mindset is why I feel my suspicions are pretty much on track.

At a funeral of one of our successful friends a year or two later, who died in a head-on collision while riding his Harley motorcycle, I introduced myself to the deceased's sister. I mentioned I knew her brother when we were kids. She said, "Oh, you went to school together?"

I said, "No, I met him through Alvin, 'Bingo', and Simon."

She said, "Oh, my... oh, my... Don't tell anyone." She didn't want her brother's reputation tarnished with their association! That night, at a memorial wake for the deceased, Alvin was there. I hadn't seen him for several years. (He was PROBABLY doing time for possession of stolen property, rumors I heard) Somebody asked him about what he'd been doing lately. He said, "Oh, I don't know. Some say that I'm a hit man, now."

For the record, I never thought of him as a hit man. Hit men got paid. Alvin was just another Dr.

Kevorkian. His was a mercy killing. One of Ted's kids must have told Alvin the conversation between their dad and I. Because Alvin said THAT loud enough <u>SO I COULD HEAR IT.</u> That's my story. **POISON.**

READ THE OTHER BOOKS BY THESE NEW AUTHORS

ABC's OF SIN (2014) by **LARRY MASSARO HIGHLY CONTROVERSIAL TOPICS! RATED PG** Over 200 different sins, LITERALLY, from abortion to zombies found in the Bible in current terms and what God says about them! From debt to VISA, the Pope to women preachers, bingo to smoking, anal sex to pornography, masturbation to sex texting, Facebook to T.V., caffeine (drug addiction) to bingo (gambling), baptism to the sinner's prayer, Al Qaeda to Zionism-topics you may never hear from the sanctified pulpit

HUCKLEBERRY FINN: ATTORNEY-AT-LAW

(2015) by **LARRY MASSARO** After his adventures in the California Gold Rush, Huckleberry returns to St. Petersburg to find Tom Sawyer is not only married, but attending a Bible college and the father of triplet boys! Huckleberry turns Harvard upside down with fame and his antics in school and his legal practice in Missouri and on the Mississippi

THE NATURAL SKINNY HEALTHCARE PLAN/THE SPARTAN STUDY (2015) by **LARRY MASSARO** Now your child doesn't have to be one of the millions of overweight American kids by naturally boosting their metabolism and immune system, thanks to a study that may have been the ancient secret to a vast superior Spartan army of the ancient Greek Empire

CHAIN OF COMMAND/ INAUGURATION DAY (2015) by **LARRY MASSARO** America is attacked on the most historic day of American political history, at the inauguration of an all female Presidential ticket

I WAS A HITMAN FOR HILLARY (2015) by **POISON. FICTION BASED ON FACT** of murder and conspiracy of over 70 murders and deaths under mysterious circumstances associated with the White House and the Whitewater Conspiracy and a law firm in Little Rock, Arkansas

THE KILLER MASSAGE MURDER (2015) by **POISON.** After falling into financial debt with student loans, Brian turns to his dark side of his schooling for financial responsibility

THE BACKHOE BANDITS (2015) by **POISON.** Kids growing up from playing cards for toys and comic books to running auto theft rings and bank robberies, and the fights in between while growing up

P.S. KEEP OUT OF THE CROSSHAIRS! (9/2015) by **LARRY MASSARO** How to write letters and e-mails to friends, relatives, and loved ones in military hot zones to help insure their safety and mental health as they return from deployment

CHASING GOD- THE BEST QUOTES OF MODERN DAY PENTECOST (2015) by **LARRY MASSARO** Quotes by some of the leading men of Pentecost and our country, such as Bro. Ron. Garrett, Bro. Vaughn Morton, Benjamin Franklin, and many more

COULD HILLARY BE THE ANTICHRIST? (2015) by **POISON.** Just the most resent facts

LOVE, POISON. (coming in 2016) by **POISON.** Love and "cat-fishing" on the Internet- this story may be adapted into a future off Broadway play